Malou in Haiti

M.K. Ayiti

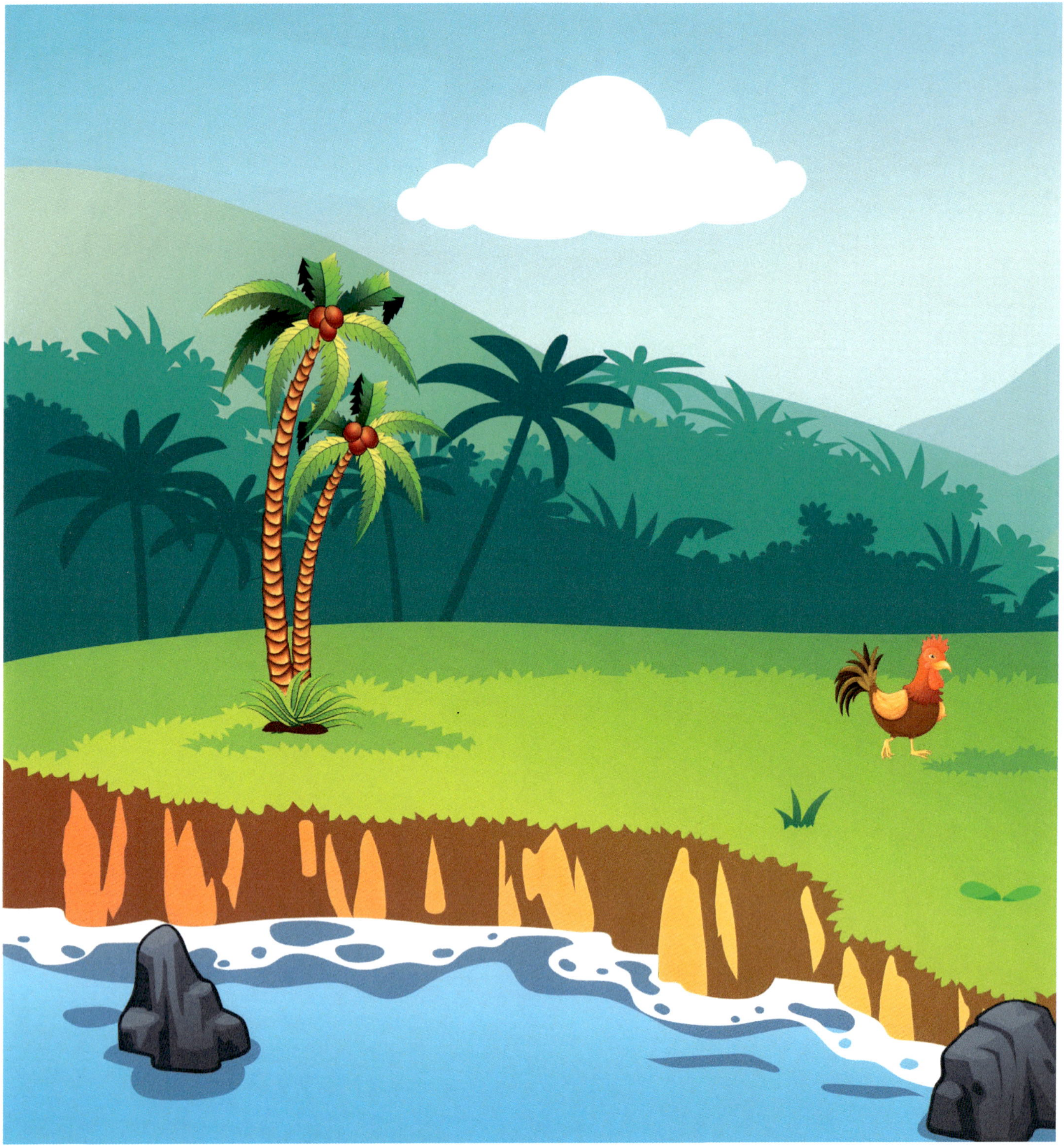

My name is Malou.

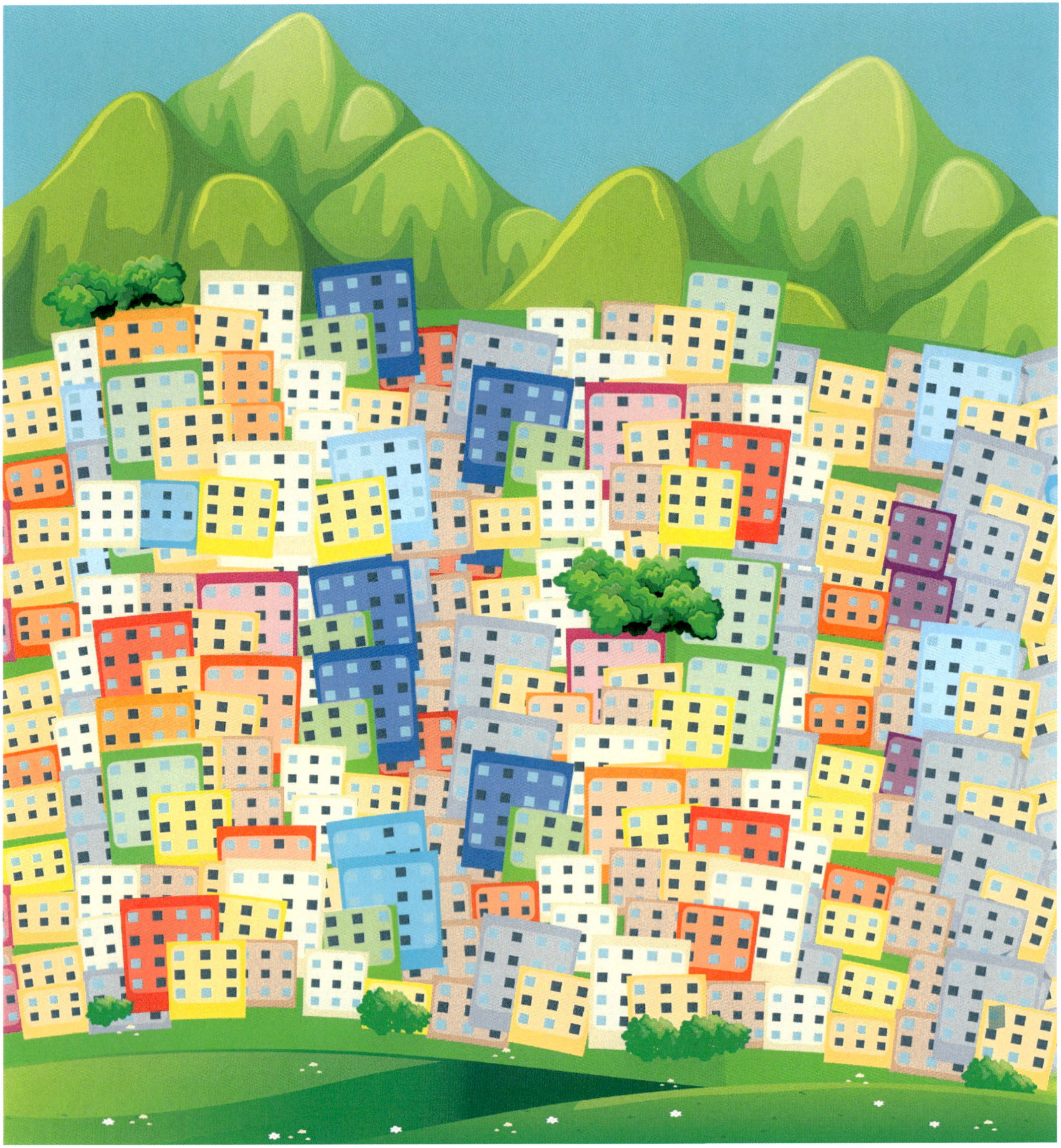

I live in Haiti.

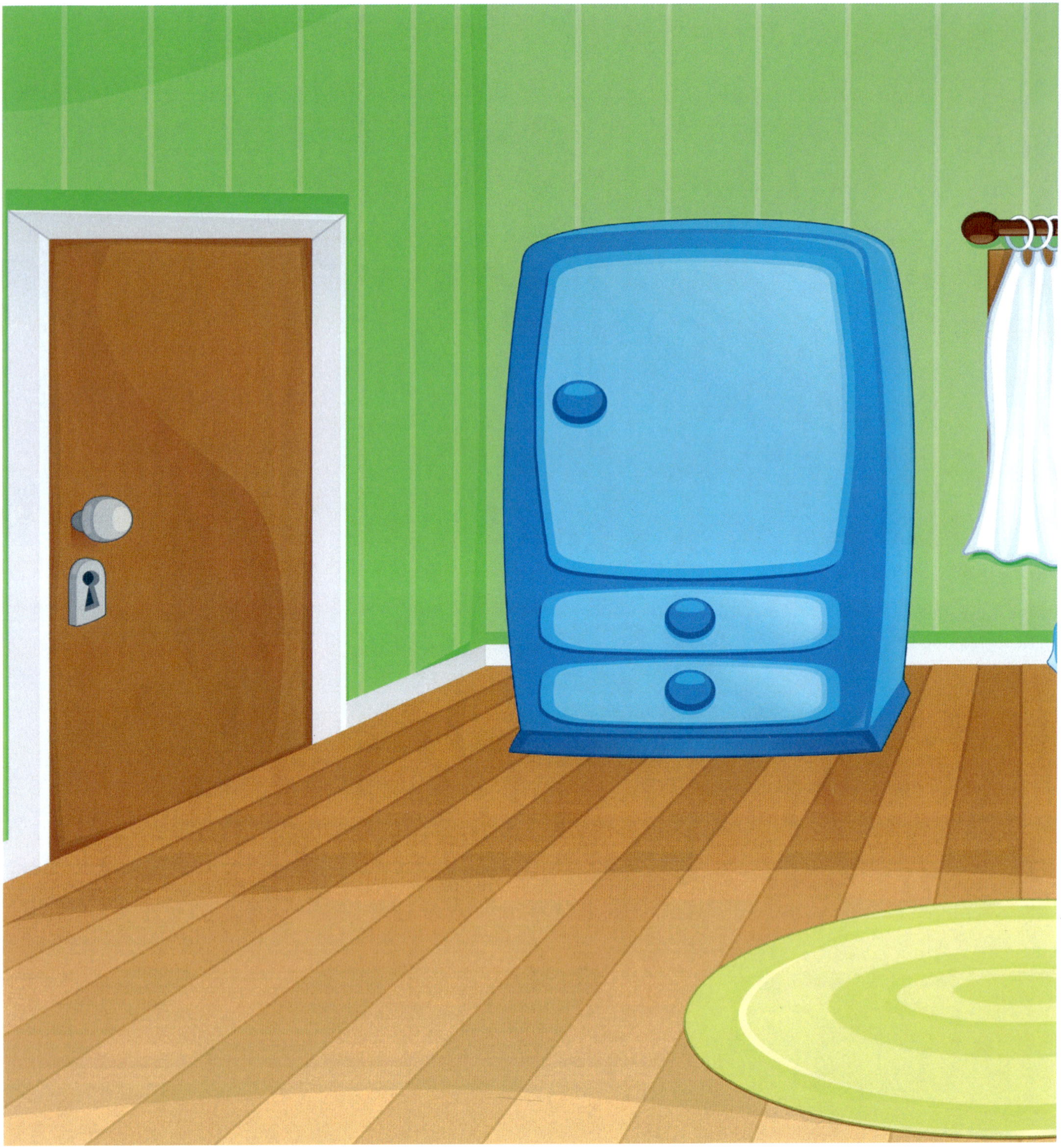

I live with my mom and dad.

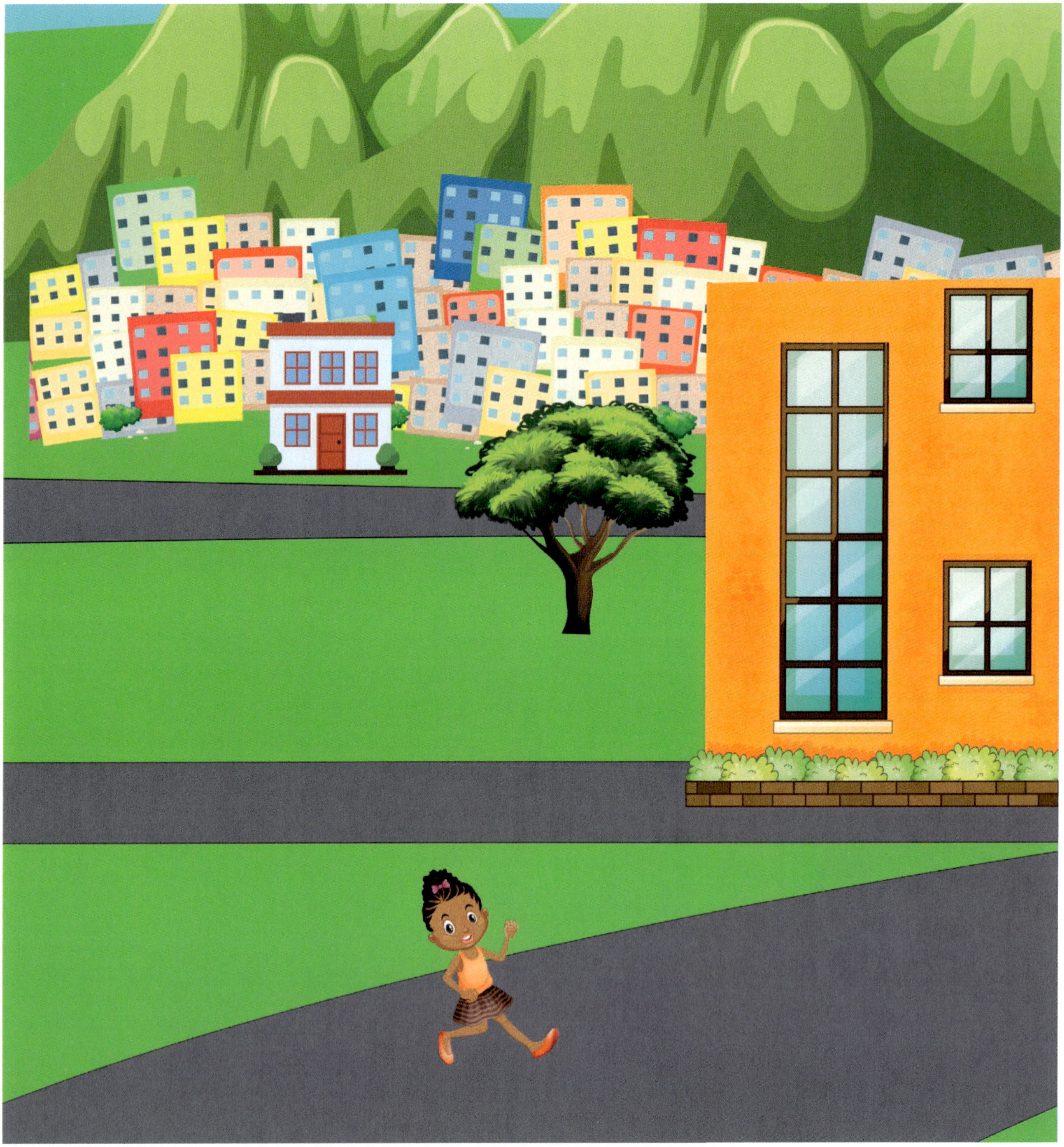

Our house is on top of a big hill.
I love to run up and down the hills.

I love to play with my friends.

We play tag and jump rope.
I am really good at jumping rope.

Haiti is a really fun place.

There are lots of beaches and mountains.

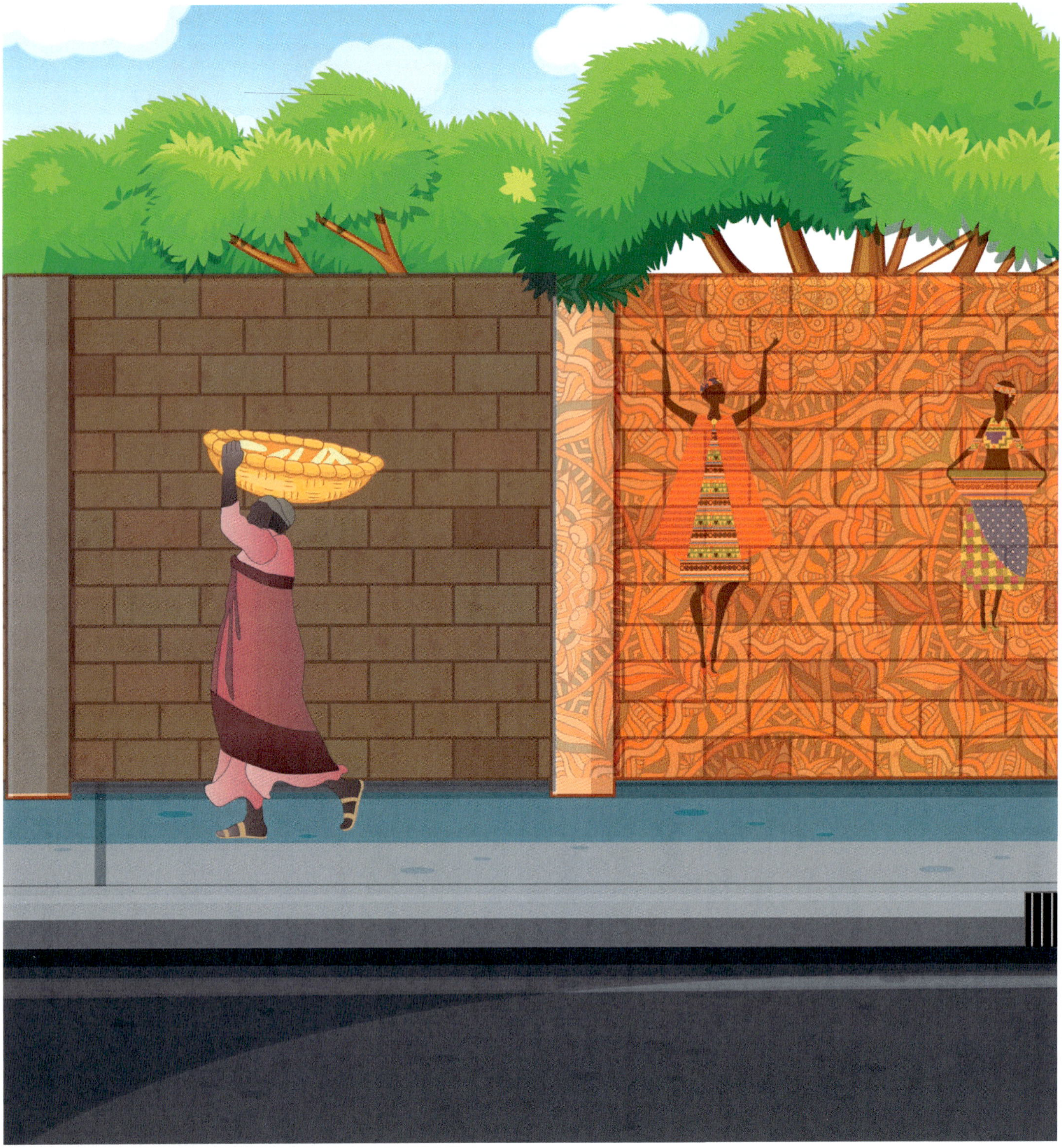

I like to look at the art painted all over the streets.

I like going to the market and buying treats.
My favorite is shaved ice.

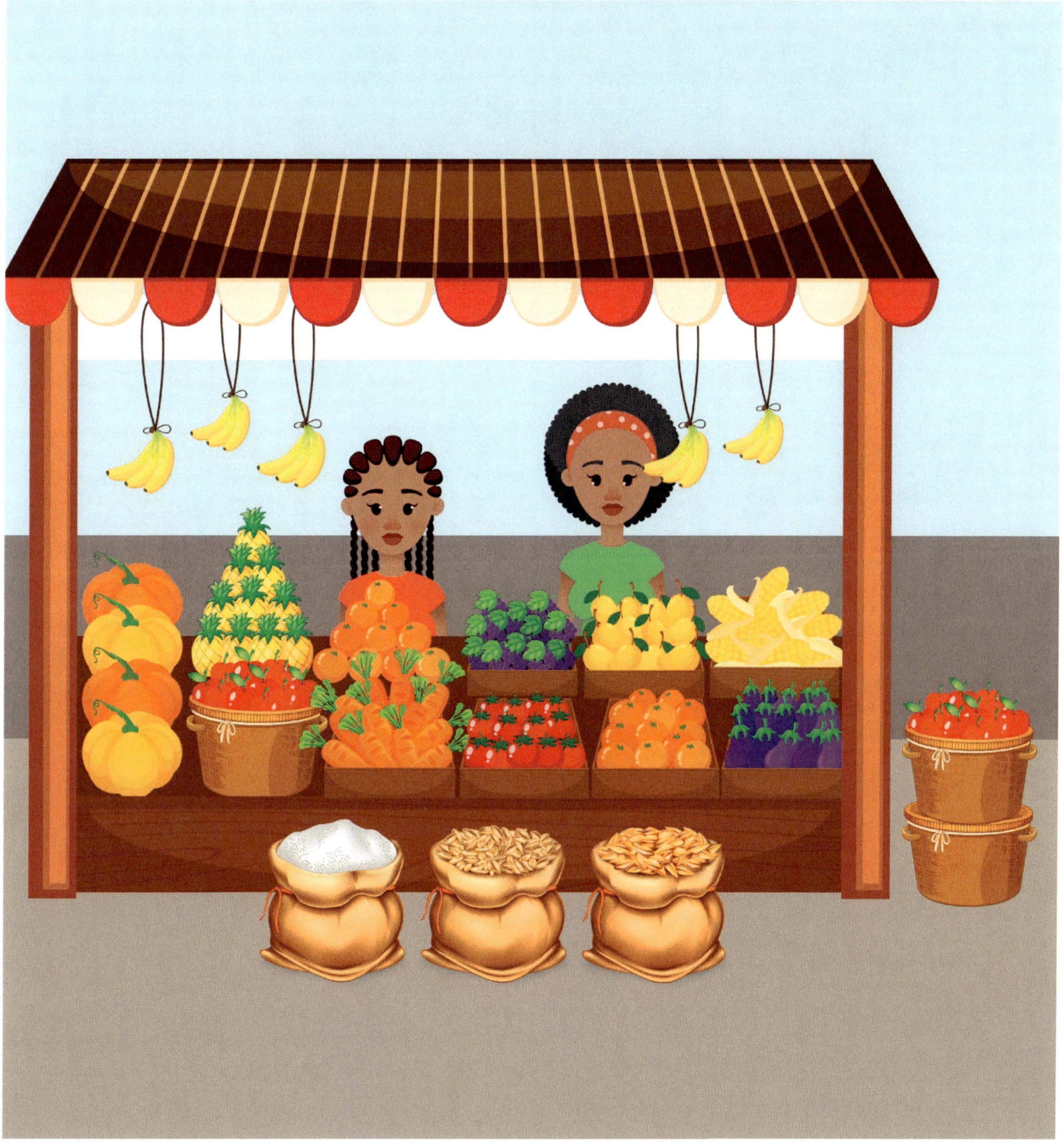

Haiti's not always perfect though.

In the summer, it gets really hot and sometimes it rains a lot.

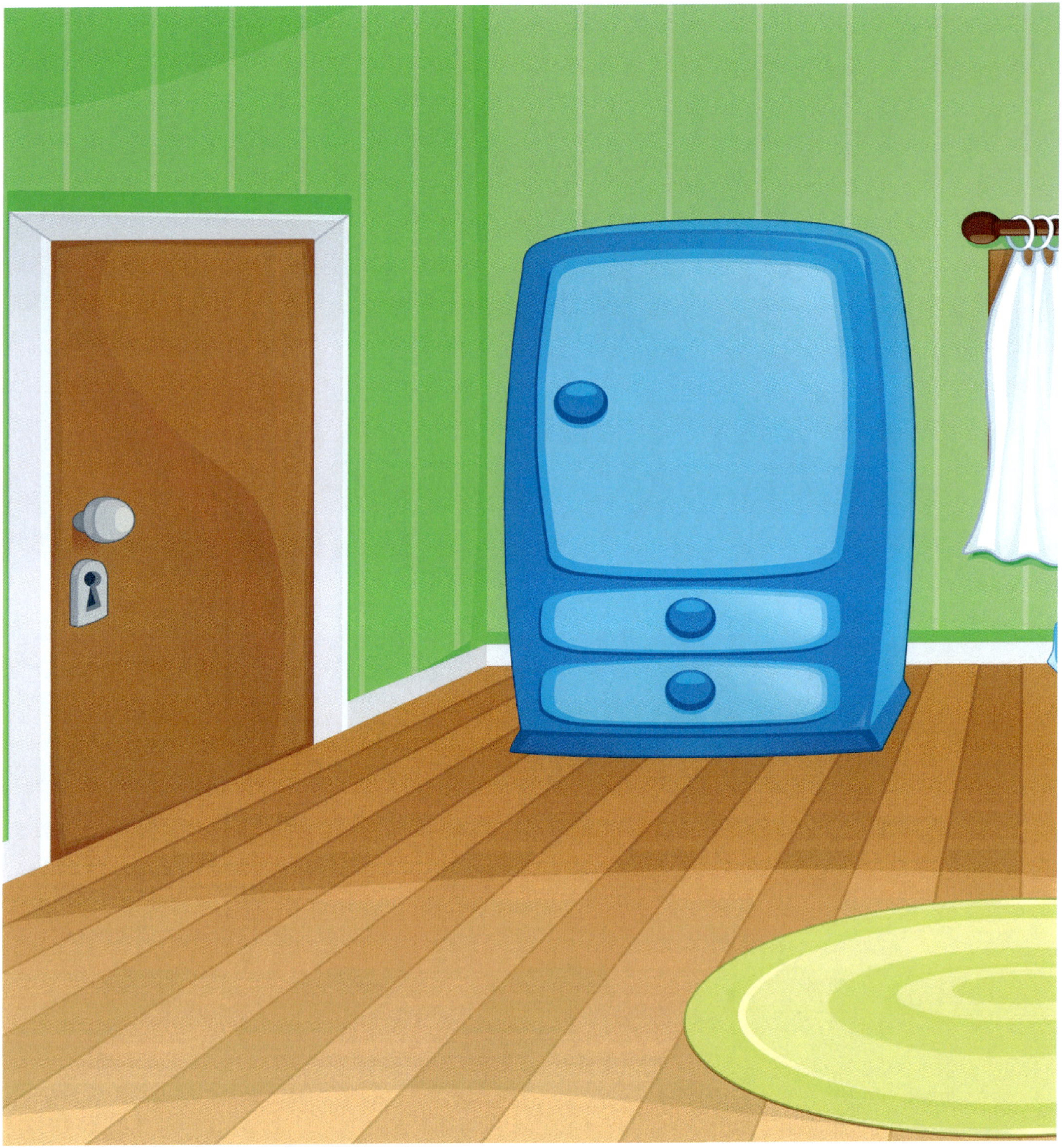

I also have to wake up early for school.

One day, my aunt and I took a taxi to school.

The taxis in Haiti are called *tap taps*. It was really fun, but the road was very bumpy.

I love my friends, my family, and my neighbors. I know almost everybody in my neighborhood.

The food is great, too. This is a Haitian mango. It's one of my favorites even though it can be messy to eat.

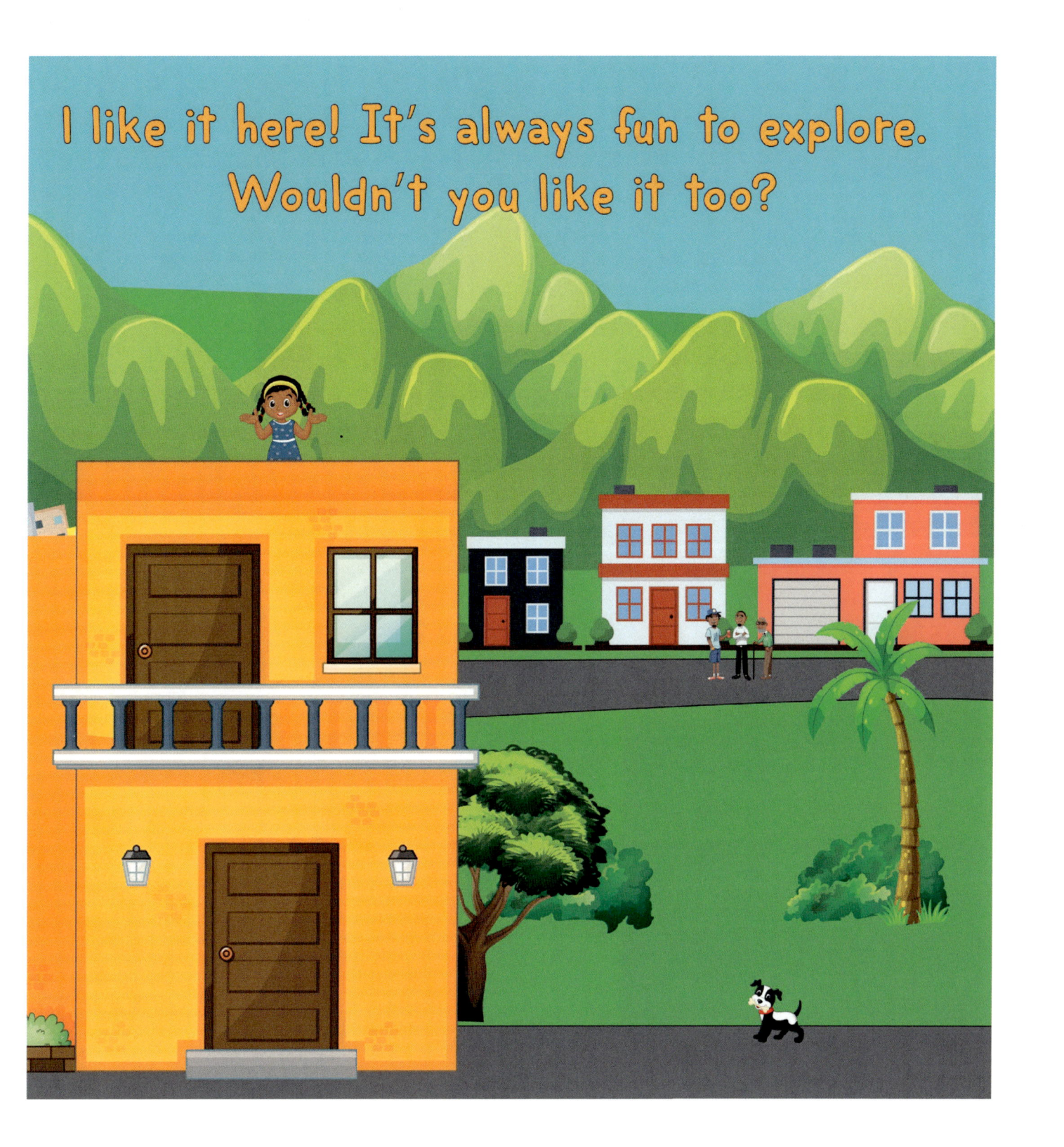

I like it here! It's always fun to explore.
Wouldn't you like it too?

Made in the USA
Coppell, TX
28 February 2024